Where Is Harry?

. . . and orders them to clean up!
I must find parents for you today. Then I will not have to put up with you anymore!
I do not want new parents. I want us to stay together.
Do not worry, Rocky.
Sly is right, Rocky. We will stay together.
Right here at Sunny Day Home.

Teddy notices that her pet is missing!
Harry is gone!
The search is on!
He is not here!
He is not in here!
They make a mess looking for Harry.
And he is not here.

Time is up.
Get down here as fast as you can!

Messy again, they slide downstairs.
Sorry!
We came as fast as we could!
Ugh!

The parents have arrived!
Welcome to the Sunny Day Home for Orphans!
Miss Crimp drags Teddy around.
This will be your last day at Sunny Day, Teddy!
She never talks! She loves to clean! She will do all your work for you!
That is nice, but we would like to keep looking.
Rocky and Sly have some fun.

TIM-BER!
You say that this girl can clean?
A couple is interested in Teddy.
We have to save Teddy!
Yes, this girl cleans like a dream!

But she does not look clean.
She is messy because she just . . . washed the roof!
But she is so tall!
That is why she can wash the roof!
Okay, we will take her. I do hate to clean.
WAIT!
Look, Teddy! There is Harry!
Who is Harry?
My spider!

Teddy leaps to Harry's rescue!
There is my pet!
Her pet?!
Hold still, Miss Crimp. We will help you.
Yes, Harry is her pet. He goes where Teddy goes!
You cannot have a spider for a pet. It is not clean.
Harry is the cleanest of all of us!
The day is saved for the misfits—and Harry!
We will always stick together!

THERE IS NO PLACE LIKE HOME

Not the attic, Miss Crimp! It is dirty there!
No, my pretty little sweets, not you!
You three— up the stairs!
Anything you say!
Sly finds a ladder.
I am going out!
Where are you going?
Shh! I can hear Miss Crimp!

I have not one but three kids for you! Come now and they are yours!
Sly tries to go back up before Miss Crimp sees him.
See you very soon! Good-bye!
Too late!
Get down here right now!
DING DONG!
Hello! Here are your perfect kids!
Is she talking about us?

It looks like good-bye, Sunny Day . . .
Darling—they need us!
We will take them!
. . . hello, perfect home!
There you go!
That is much better!
Eat up!
But do not spill!
I cannot even swallow!

So can we play? Run? Jump?
Do anything?

Oh, no!
You will get messed up!

Have a cookie!
But be neat!

Well, time for bed.
Good idea!
You will sleep like perfect angels!
I cannot take it! Even the cookies are perfect!
We have to get out of here!
I am with you!
I have it! We can all get what we want!
What do you mean "all"?
You will see!

While the perfect parents are sleeping . . .
GRRR!
Run!
At least the dog likes perfect cookies!
Whew!

Back at Sunny Day Home:
They are great for you! They are *perfect*!
You are going to love it!
KNOCK-KNOCK
You are even more perfect today!
The perfect kids—just what we wanted!
Oh, no, Miss Crimp, we have our perfect kids!
It looks like those three will get to stay with you!

A NEW HOME SWEET HOME

Who could be at the door?
A new one? Today of all days!
What a little mess!
He will ruin the pretty party!
Oh, no, he will not! He will sit here and not move! Let us go, my sweets!!

The parents arrive.
Welcome to Sunny Day Home! You can take a kid, but you cannot take a flower—those are mine!

All I want is a home sweet home . . . !

You sing well!

I do not know why we cannot just walk up the stairs.
What is your name?
Brad.

Do not worry. We will take care of you!
You bet!

You are kind. But all I want is my own home.
I have it!
Oh, boy.
The misfits have an idea!
Boy, is it hot out here!
I am so tired!
Ice Cream

How about I give you a rest *and* sell all that ice cream?
Ice Cr
Kid, you have a deal.
There is ice cream out back!
Do you really mean it?
Sly gives Teddy the signal . . .

. . . and Teddy puts Brad on the porch!
You can do it, Brad! Sing!
♪
We want that one!
No, give him to us!
But he is a mess! I cannot believe they want him!
We will give you a home.

Wait!
I have more kids! Nice kids! Clean kids!
But they are all a mess!
Never mind!
There are no more kids today! Thank you for coming!
It is a sweet ending for everyone! Well, almost everyone.
Thank you, Miss Crimp!